Stories from the Towers of Stone and Steel

Stories from the Towers of Stone and Steel

Written and illustrated by Jason Buck

Jason Buck
2016

First Printing: 2016

ISBN: 978-1-326-72678-2

Jason Buck

www.JasonBuckStoryTeller.co.uk

Contents

Acknowledgements.. vii

Foreword ix

Ink.. 11

The Unluckiest Man on the Brass Coast 47

Dream Eater... 73

Swipe Right... 83

The Onion Man 87

Acknowledgements

Thanks to Matt Pennington and Profound Decisions for the use of the name of the fantasy land 'The Brass Coast'.

Thanks to Mayu Nakamura for her helping me understand the dream eating Baku and for bringing the horrific Umibōzu into my life.

Thanks to the man in the street with the tattooed face, who smiled and let me take his photograph, and who ultimately inspired the story Ink and was so clearly 'Danny'.

Thanks to Louise and my son Oskar for frank feedback and constant encouragement, and thanks to Oskar for his illustration (Akiko's picture) of the Baku.

Lastly, thanks to Tessa, James and all the Canadians, English, Irish and Scots for letting me finish this, even though we were all supposed to be on holiday together.

Foreword

Stories, legends and fairy tales so often start in forests, on windswept mountains or any number of places in nature. This book contains, instead, stories that are set or begin in cities or towns – places where so many of us live these days and where just as much magic can happen.

Like the first book in this series, 'Stories from the Woods and Wild Places', these stories were originally written for telling out loud and have all been performed for live audiences.

The story 'Ink', in this book, has been extended so it's more like a short literary story, rather than something for telling, but should you wish to tell it, just pick out the main points and join it together in your own way.

There was another story that didn't make the cut. The trouble with stories is you need to let them write themselves and just trying to stitch together some good ideas does not a story make. When it's ready, when it's written itself and been cooked properly it'll be included in a book. Until then, only my favourites and the best have made the cut.

Ink

This man lived in Camden.

He'd been born in Nottingham, gone to school in Nottingham, still had most of his family in Nottingham, but had moved to London in his early twenties.

He hadn't been very good at schoolwork. It was difficult and it bored him. He'd had particular trouble with what others saw as the simple tasks of reading and writing. In adult life he'd wondered if he was dyslexic, but his Mum and Dad hadn't known much about that, so he just settled for being what *they* described as 'thick'. Anyway, if anyone had tried to make him feel bad about his 'lack of academic achievement' – not his words, you understand – he could just make a joke out of it. If that didn't work he had two convincing arguments with which to silence people, both clenched at the end of each arm, whenever they were needed.

Easy.

None of this mattered: He was going to be a rock star – a heavy metal rock star – or at least somehow be involved in heavy metal music. He and his mates had all grown their hair, contrary to the school rules, wore leather biker jackets, contrary to the school rules, and had their ears pierced, contrary to the school rules and much to the dismay of their Mums who moaned about them ruining their bodies, and to the horror of their Fathers who muttered darkly about *poofs*.

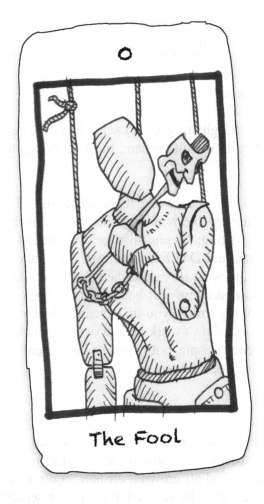

The Fool

He and some of his mates had set up a band, variously called 'Chainsaw Desolation', 'Suicide Death' and 'Zombie something-or-other'. They rehearsed a bit and nearly got a gig on the basement stage at Rock City because the drummer's girl-friend worked in the bar there. The lead singer now lived in Newbury, wherever that was, and was something high up in insurance.

As well as his music, he'd also loved art: T-shirts, posters, patches embroidered with album covers that could be sewn onto sleeveless denim jackets that would, in turn, go over a biker jacket. Fantasy art and gothic or death metal artwork were his favourites; sketches, scribbles and doodles involving demons, dragons, fire and a lot of skulls and Grim Reapers, filled the back pages of most of his exercise books. He'd liked art but, actually, wasn't really very good at drawing – something that became apparent as he got older and suddenly there were people in his group of friends who were off to Art College. Now, some of *those* guys could really draw and he got them to paint his leather. Big, sweeping gothic grotesques: A skeletal biker, wreathed in fire on the jacket's back, and a lot of smaller designs, collected over time, down each arm and across his shoulders. He was proud of that leather – *still* proud to wear it, twenty years on, the weathering, scuffs and cracks, in his mind, only adding to the provenance of its authenticity (also not his words).

When most of his friends had gone away to university, and often stayed in those cities, or charity-shopped their black and thinning sleeveless t-shirts, cut their hair and got jobs as the corporate slaves they'd once professed they'd rather die than be, or had become mothers and fathers and never seen again, indentured to their darling spawn and forbidden from entering a pub after 3pm, he decided to go with a friend to join a house-share near Camden in London, and find his fortune in the Capital's Mecca for the Alternative Lifestyle tribes.

1

The Magician

So, now, this man, Marc, lived in Camden.

Of course, bills needed to be paid, and in the absence of any roadie work, Marc got a job as a delivery driver for one of the big couri-

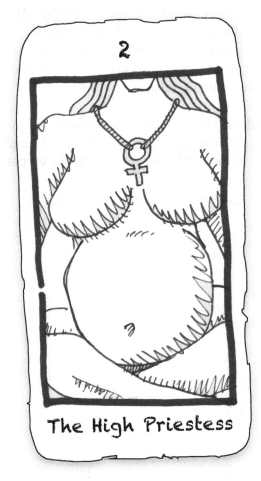

The High Priestess

er firms. There was the occasional early morning - but that was paid overtime - and they let him wear his hair long, if he tied it back in a ponytail. He wasn't going to sell out.

Now in his forties and fully immersed in the soup of London's alty lifestyle, where conventional attitudes and fashions were rejected and a uniform of identical dark clothing, brands and accepted music, game or film merchandise were worn to show this individuality, Marc got his first tattoo.

The tattoo studio was just off Camden High Street. He'd been toying with the idea for years, and recommendations from some of his friends who already had tattoos had made him think why not go and have a look?

Like many tattoo studios, the windows of 'Danny's Urban Tattoo's and Piercing's' were blanked out. A curling, bichromatic script announced the name, surmounted by coiling Chinese dragons with staring eyes and flaring nostrils. Close-up photos of recent work showed arms and backs, breasts and bellies, buttocks, calves and thighs with shiny new ink jobs, surrounded by halo of angry, pink skin and all next to a sign declaring "No tattoos on face, neck or hands".

Reassured, Marc opened the door and entered a new world.

There was an air of pseudo-orientalism: Bubbling tanks stuffed with bobbing bubble-eye goldfish, vacuum-molded, ceramic Chinese demigods hefted ornate halberds and glowered through spiraling moustaches and blue-shadowed eyes, a Japanese katana longsword was mounted high on the wall, over the multi-coloured, plastic strip-curtain that lead into the actual studio, and out of reach of grasping hands, while a heavy pawl of habitual incense filled the air.

"Can I help you?" asked the woman behind the counter.

Maybe she was Danny? Danny – like Dannii Minogue? Either way, Marc thought she was beautiful: Young, early to mid twenties, long jet black hair with a scarlet streak and a severe fringe. Great makeup – just like a proper metal chick – dark, gothic and dramatic, her blood-red, black-outlined lipstick accented with two, tiny, jeweled studs in both her upper and lower lips. Looked like a great figure under that black t-shirt, and were those contacts she was wearing? They must be – no one really had eyes *that* colour.

"You alright?" the woman asked, smiling at Marc's staring, enjoying his boyish discomfort as he stuttered.

"I was just thinking about, maybe, getting a tattoo".

"Do you know what sort of thing you're after?" she said, turning her attention to polishing one of her already highly polished nails, the same colour as her lips.

"Um. Not really", he began, starting to feel foolish. "I've got a few ideas, but ...", he trailed off.

"Well, have a look at some of those", she suggested, pointing at display boards, mounted on hinges against a wall, like train time tables on a station platform.

Marc went over and started to leaf through the boards, enjoying pouring over the designs, new and familiar: Spiky tribal abstracts; Grim Reapers with scythes and various messages in horror show scripts; panthers whose claws dug into the design with little red blood trails so it appeared – a weak illusion – that they climbed up the flesh of the owner; Chinese dragons; Tolkien style dragons; disproportionately busty mermaids; Priapic Smurfs; bat-winged and fork-tailed curvy succubae, blowing kisses; knives; swords; axes; Jimi Hendrix puffing thick smoke out of his mouth; Elvis; Pokémon; Jesus ... an unending variety and contrast, between the elegant or dramatic and the prosaic or crude.

After a while it reached a point where he couldn't take in any more. He'd seen many designs he liked, and many he didn't, but he was still far from making any sort of decision. It must have shown.

"Sleep on it", said the woman, with a smile. "Only get one when you're sure".

He smiled back.

"I will", he said and, thanking her, left.

Over the next couple of weeks he popped in for a few minutes, between shifts or after work, to look at the designs again and again. He was always the only one in the front of the shop, although often there was the buzz of the tattoo needle from the back, where the master was at work.

Being the only person there meant he got to find out a bit more about the tattooing process. He didn't like the idea of a needle injecting him hundreds of times a second but, as he got told, a big strong man like him was "hard enough to handle it". These words of encouragement came, always, from the Rock Chick at the desk. Sable was her name – if it was her real name or not, Marc didn't care; he was enthralled. She was incredibly sexy – something you'd normally only find on the internet. And she knew all about the stuff that he and his friends liked: The music, the games, the films, the places to go. And she laughed at his rubbish, shy jokes and made him feel sexy and cool.

He had made some subtle enquiries as to Sable's relationship status. Nothing forward or likely to spoil their growing, albeit pro-fessional, friendship but, you know … just in case. Very quickly, she had announced, "I'm Danny's", with a sad little smile, jerking her head towards the plastic strip-curtain, behind which the inter-mittent buzzing of the needle could be heard.

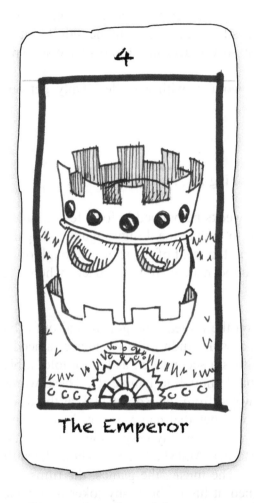

The Emperor

Finally, Marc began to feel that he was coming to a decision about his tattoo-to-be. It was going to be a design that wasn't off the shelf, but based on similar designs he'd seen in the shop: It was going to be a Grim Reaper, his scythe curling over His cowled skull with flames curling up off the top of the blade's arc, bearing the words "You're mine".

He was reminded of all the Grammar Nazi pictures on the internet, showing misspellings on tattoos – especially of your / you're – and made a mental note to check it with someone who was good at that sort of thing.

He even bought a plain paper exercise book, unwittingly reliving his school days by drawing and redrawing his idea. He never showed anyone these – he could see they weren't good enough to look at. Besides, there was the odd fantasy picture of Sable in there too and so the book was firmly self-suppressed, hidden between two hard backs on a shelf in his room in his shared house.

And then, one weekend, things changed.

As had become traditional over the years, on Saturday nights he and a bunch of like-minded alternative mates would meet at the World's End, just near the tube station. It was always rammed, but that was part of the fun, feeling the energy of the crowd – the crowd that was your world, everyone getting pumped up and ready for a night of clubbing. You had to get the balance right and leave close enough to 11pm, before the crowd started to build up a turgid queue outside the club, but also not so early that you were the first into an empty and vacuous dark space, where the music you'd enjoy later echoed off the black walls and you were very aware of just how much your feet stuck to the floor.

Perfect timing, yet again, and there were only a few youngsters clogging up the queue outside the Electric Ballroom. It was 'Full Tilt' night and like a zombie apocalypse, people arrived in couples or ragged groups, converging like the incoming tide, on the alternative night club. Black leather jackets were more for Marc and his Old Skool friends, whereas the predominating

The Hierophant

younger patrons were more of the cyberpunk / cybergoth era: Baggy trousers, meeting the floor, despite the metal banded, three inch soles of their boots; skin-tight tops for both sexes; long flowing black coats and hair styles from shaved to fountains of neon dreadlock extensions, carefully woven into bleach-tattered cascades of hair. And piercings. Lots of piercings and tattoos on show.

After the traditional straight double gin shot in one of the upstairs bars, where Marc and his friends always marveled at how the colourless spirit shone a ghostly purple in the black lights, it was back onto the beer and then into the watching. Marc didn't like to dance. He didn't feel he was any good at it, and instead preferred to lounge at the edge of the room, stony faced, watching the pretty young girls twirling, and chuntering with his friends about the state of the young men. But this was what it was all about. It was about being part of the scene and he loved it.

At some point not long after midnight, when everyone was pleasantly pissed, but before things got messy, there was great excitement among his friends and Marc was told that he had to "meet this guy".

It turned out that "this guy" was Danny.

Ok, he was impressed. Danny was a big bloke, muscular and, although not particularly tall, carried himself in such a way as to give an air of charisma and strength. He was probably in his midforties, about the same age as Marc, shaved head and a ragged, goatee that was streaked with early grey. He had the regulation heavy boots, but the leather trousers looked expensive and fitted him perfectly. A simple white, long sleeved top was under an old–looking leather waistcoat and all of this topped by a long, soft leather coat – again this looked well made and fitted the man well, reminiscent of the surcoat of a Black Knight.

And, oh, the tattoos. Beautifully and sparingly deployed, they peeked out from the neck and sleeves of his top – hints of licking tongues of flame and the tails of great mythical reptiles. While Danny's neck was uninscribed, one half of his face and hairless, shaved head was etched with geometric lines, dog-legging in triangular corners and sweeping in spirals, to follow the contours of his skull, like a Maori warrior.

But the finishing touch that made Danny's entrance wasn't his clothing, his tattoos, or even Danny himself. It was Sable. She curled out from behind him, like a cat, allowing Danny to run one large hand from the back of her head, down her back to rest on the upper curve of her buttocks.

Sable spotted Marc. Her eyes widened and her mouth opened in a theatrically surprised smile. Danny stared impassively at the quiet metaller in front of him, apparently waiting for someone else to start the conversation.

Some of Marc's friends twittered around Danny and Sable, ingratiating themselves and eventually introducing Marc, before being cut off by the young female.

"I know who *this* is", she smiled coyly, turning to Danny. "This is the guy I told you about who's been thinking about getting a piece done. I've been helping him make up his mind, haven't I?"

She cupped Marc's chin in her hand. He was acutely aware that this was the first time they'd made any form of physical contact and he was both very uncomfortable and excited.

Danny's face softened and he smiled.

"Good to meet you", he said loudly over the music, extending his free, right hand. "When you've made your mind up, come and see me. I think I know what'd look good on a fella like you".

Marc's attention was now absorbed by Danny. He was the real deal. He was proper rock-and-roll.

"I think I know what I want", Marc shouted, leaning forward to be nearer, so Danny didn't have to.

"Oh yeah?" replied the artist. "Tell me what you're thinking", he continued. "And what are you drinking?"

So Marc sat down with Danny who, it turned out was *totally* rock-and-roll. Like Marc, he'd left school with close to nothing in terms of qualifications, started a band, but found he was better at being a roadie and had toured with some of the big names in metal, back in the late 80s. He'd been taught tattooing by an old guy with a similar history and connections to some really big names from the 60s and 70s.

Danny also referred to himself as a *Chromatathurge*, which didn't mean much to Marc, but it sounded like a lot of the Pagan beliefs and religions that a lot of people he knew followed. Again, this was something Danny had apparently learned from his mentor and meant, so he said, that he lived a satisfying and rich life.

Marc, in return, talked about his aspirations, how he'd wanted to be involved with music and the metal scene since he was a young teenager, how he felt he'd give *anything* to have a proper rock-and-roll lifestyle and how he'd been true to the way of life and not sold out.

During this audience with the great Danny, Sable flitted between dancing on her own – and clearly rebuffing approaches by many men, all watched from the side-lines by Danny, who only once had to fix one young man with a stare and slowly shake his head – fetching drinks for the two men and hovering around *her* man. Once or twice, she'd decided to sit on Marc's lap, making him feel very awkward – not only because he'd had to politely lean around one or other side of her to hear Danny, but also because he'd had to shift position so she couldn't feel quite how awkward she actually made him feel.

Marc's circle of friends was very impressed.

Eventually, the early hours came and closing time approached.

"Some people are coming back after, if you fancy it?" asked Danny.

"Oh yes, you've got to come", giggled Sable. Again, far too flirty for what Marc was used to, but as Danny just smiled indulgently, he supposed it was all great fun. The gin and a lot of beer probably helped too.

It turned out that Danny and Sable lived in the floors above the tattoo studio. It was only about ten minutes' wobbly walk from the club and a noisy crowd of about fifteen of them – some Marc knew, some he didn't – sang and swaggered along together, arms around each others' shoulders. The London streets, almost as busy at kick out time as they had been earlier, were filled with similar people, all in various states of drunkenness – big groups or newly formed couples, all bleeding out of the heart of the city. This was what it was all meant to be about.

Leaving the main street and entering the quieter side streets, they went in through a door at the side of the studio. Yes, they could get to the flat *through* the studio, but Danny said there was

6

The Lovers

no way he was going to drag a rowdy group through his sterile and expensively equipped work space.

In the living quarters above the shop, Marc was quickly seduced by the memorabilia mounted on the walls, the weapons hung in racks, state-of-the-art sound system, an almost wall-length aquarium containing brightly coloured tropical marine fish and corals, large squishy sofas and a huge flat screen.

As he was goggling at this Alternative's Heaven, Danny started handing out tinnies and someone pressed a beer into his hand. Music blasted into life and Marc sank into a sofa, feeling he'd made it this time. For a while he just sipped and looked about, feeling he was in some sort of gallery. Near him, someone had lit a joint and, even though he didn't smoke, the strong herby aroma only helped to make him feel he ought to relax and enjoy the late evening.

He'd been watching Danny for a little while, stirring something steaming in a mug when he walked over and offered it to Marc.

"It's what the South American shaman use to help them see into the 'other reality'", he explained. "Tastes like mud, but I make it weak so it does give you some visuals, but you don't lose it altogether". He smiled, and held out the mug for Marc to take.

He was among friends. He'd met this very cool guy. He might never be in this place doing these things with these people ever again. Why not?

He sipped the hot liquid. Danny was right, it did taste like mud, but, to be honest, not a lot worse than some of the herbal teas some of his more earthy friends tried to foist on him.

"Drink it all", said Danny encouragingly and with an expert air. So Marc did.

Danny took the empty mug back, smiled at Marc and said, "I'll be back in a few minutes and then we can really talk about your tattoo".

A few minutes later, Marc was having full visuals.

The already crowded and noisy room seemed to have even more people in it. Well, perhaps 'people' was the wrong word. Some of the new 'people' seemed to have animal heads, others had bodies that were shaped in ways that really shouldn't work and some of the autographed posters on the walls had been singing to him and whispering things he couldn't quite hear and was glad of that.

Whilst talking about his Reaper tattoo idea, Danny's own tattoos had started to move and crawl around his face like snakes, his eyes had gone from a deep brown to a bottomless black and when he opened his mouth to speak, it sounded like his words came from a well or a deep chasm in the ground, vibrating with ancient subterranean echoes. Meanwhile, Sable's frequent interruptions with more beer, strokes from Danny, or flirtations with Marc were no less distracting than the fact he felt he could almost, on the edge of his consciousness and vision, see batwings and a forked tail on the girl and this certainly made her no less attractive.

At some point Marc had got up to use the loo, which was an interestingly psychedelic experience in itself. After staring at himself in the bathroom mirror and deciding that wasn't going to end well, seeing as his face moved and changed, like lapping waves at low tide, he opened the door to return to the party only to find his way blocked.

Sable was standing in the corridor, just outside.

"Oh, um, sorry," started Marc, embarrassed at being in such close quarters with the young woman when no one else was around. Moving to one side to let Sable into the bathroom he leaned his back against a door, so as to give her plenty of room. He avoided her eyes, until again she cupped his chin in one small hand, her long, curved and brightly varnished nails digging into the flesh of his cheeks as she lifted his face to look at hers.

He was really stoned. Those contacts – those eyes – were unreal, the sweep of her cheekbones and the curve of her lips as they parted in a smile, the thick, deep red lipstick sticking them together slightly. He was feeling light headed for all sorts of reasons and was completely off guard when she pushed him gently, but very firmly in the chest, opening the door he was leaning against and

7

The Chariot

sending him staggering back into the dark room, falling backwards onto a bed.

He propped himself up on his elbows.

"And this is the guest room", drawled Sable against the background noise of the party elsewhere in the building, sweeping her arm around her proprietorially and sounding like a mockery of a TV house show presenter. She stood in the light of the open doorway, curves and hair silhouetted in perfect black.

She leaned on one hip and flicked her hair, her forked tail swishing from side to side like an angry cat, and there was the thick sound of a zip opening against the strain of skin-tight denim.

* * *

When he woke next morning, Marc had trouble remembering the later events of the previous evening.

He was in a strange bed in a strange room, now seeing it in the light, which brought about a level of detail that hadn't been available to him when he'd crashed out last night.

Oh God.

Last night.

Sable.

Well, he was alone. Naked, yes, but alone.

His head thumped, he was painfully dehydrated, he certainly hadn't had enough sleep and his right forearm ached.

Ok … time to face the day, face the music. Whatever. He was too hung over to take anything too seriously at the moment, beyond his own discomfort.

Rock-and-roll.

It was only when he sat up and swiveled to sit on the edge of the bed and recover his underwear, that the question of why his forearm hurt occurred to him. He looked down at it, wincing as it felt like his dried out brain rolled around in his skull. His right forearm had been mostly shaved, at least on the upper side and now had what looked like clingfilm fixed in place with surgical tape covering the part that hurt. Clearly visible through the transparent plastic membrane was what was unmistakably a tattoo. He pulled on his shorts, jeans, socks and boots, feeling his eyes bulge with the pressure as he leant forward to lace them. He pulled on his t-shirt, smelling of last night's secondary smoke and old sweat, laced with a pervasive undercurrent of perfume. This brought back memories that were both welcome and worrying. What was going to happen if he encountered Sable or, worse, Danny? But then he wanted to know what the hell had happened on his arm!

Dressed, he stood, calibrating his balance, still drunk and probably still suffering from whatever had been in that mug.

Opening the door, he looked down the carpeted corridor. Everything was deafeningly quiet now, but a smell of fresh coffee reached him, making his stomach rumble with hunger. Taking a deep breath, he plunged on, towards where he thought he could remember the living room was, in search of answers and, more importantly, his biker leather.

Justice

Entering the living room, he was pleased to see he wasn't the only casualty of the night. Half a dozen puffy-eyed hangover victims looked up and nodded at him, doing their best to smile a greeting without causing themselves too much pain.

"The sleeper awakes!" Danny was sat in a corner at a small dining table, feet up on another chair. He was dressed in a white t-shirt and board shorts, grinning at Marc and seeming no worse for wear, unlike his guests.

"Coffee?" he asked, nodding to a huge cafetiere on the table, accompanied by a carton of milk and surrounded by a huddle of clean, empty mugs, before sipping his own steaming brew.

Marc nodded and grunted in what he hoped was welcome agreement. He wasn't sure how much Danny knew about what had happened with him and Sable. He simultaneously felt guilty for abusing the hospitality of his host (and a very cool guy), and like he was walking on air and ready to skip off into the sunset with The Girl of His Dreams.

After scooping up his leather and draping it on the arm of a sofa, he poured a mug of black coffee and took a sip, before noticing his arm again.

"What's this?" he asked.

"You don't remember?" Danny replied, enjoying a slight smile.

"I think there's quite a bit of last night I don't remember".

"I bet you say that to all the girls", replied to Danny with a wolfish grin, rising to his feet. His comment didn't make Marc feel any better, but both painfully and thankfully, Sable was nowhere to be seen at the moment.

Danny lifted Marc's arm with an air of professional inspection.

"You", he began, as he gently peeled the tape off, and started to remove the clingfilm, "decided last night, that it was now or never".

"Wha-?" started Marc, but Danny continued.

"I don't usually do work for people when they're pissed, but I know you'd already come to a decision and you asked me to design something for you. So I did this".

Danny had now peeled off the tape and the plastic covering, and had taken a sterile wipe from a pack on the table. Despite the stinging, he was wiping away a thin crust of dried blood to reveal a beautiful rendition of a tarot card: The Wheel of Fortune.

It was metal, it was steampunk, it was gothic. The detail was superb, the colours vibrant in their newness. The image of the card was slightly and deliberately cockeyed as if lying, casually tossed onto a table – Marc's arm. The shadow behind it made it pop, as if there was a card, really there, resting on his arm. The subtle fronds? Vines? Creepers? Somethings … that just peeked out from behind the card, stretching outwards were a nice touch.

"It's amazing. It's beautiful", murmured Marc. "But …"

"I know. It's not what you originally had in mind. We'll get to that design, in time. You're going to be a canvas for the most amazing skin art the world has ever seen. I've been waiting to meet the right person – someone who wants it. Who really wants it, hungers for it, *needs* it."

"And you did this and we talked about all this canvas stuff last night?"

9

Ex-Army
Homeless
God Bless

The Hermit

"Yeah", said Danny, but Marc felt he avoided his eyes. "*'I'd give anything for a proper rock-and-roll lifestyle'* – your words, not mine, Marc. Remember? And here's your opportunity".

Danny paused, looking directly at Marc. "Sable tells me you guys talked about if for quite a while, later on". He held his gaze, with a slight, questioning smile, until Marc's eyelids fluttered and he looked away.

"Oh", was all he could say.

"So!" said Danny jumping up and grinning. "I'll be seeing you soon about the next part of the process – the next cards. Just keep this one clean and rub some E45 cream into it, morning and evening, until any scabbing has completely gone".

Marc felt overwhelmed and lacking in control of the situation, but he felt this was his cue to leave, so thanked his host, muttered some more appreciation for the tattoo – suddenly asking how much he owed Danny, only to have his question dismissed and waved a goodbye to the other recovering revelers who also seemed to understand that it was time to leave.

He trotted down the stairs from the flat to the ground level front door, opening it and drinking in the fresh outside air and made his way home, confused.

* * *

It was two or three days before he'd have time to go back to the studio and he was bursting to see Sable. He needed to know quite what had happened – he remembered quite a bit of detail from after she'd pushed him into the guest bedroom, but it had all seemed, rather cinematically, to fade to black once they'd got started, and then he'd woken up alone with a new tattoo he hadn't really planned on.

He also desperately wanted to see her. He hadn't felt like this, since he'd been a very young man. It was almost a physical pain: A feeling like a pull

The Wheel of Fortune

11

Strength

from the pit of his stomach.

He spent all day, driving for work, thinking up excuses for visiting her. He replayed events – real and imagined – from the other night, ending up with him heroically rescuing her from some interloper, or stealing her away from a doomed relationship with Danny. Every time his phone buzzed he hoped it was her, even though she didn't have his number and he dared not make the first move to contact her online, in case it aroused suspicion or got her into trouble. But then he'd get to that thing she'd said a while back. What were her words? "*I'm Danny's*", she'd said. But it wasn't like he owned her or anything. But then, again, what did he, Marc, have to offer her that Danny didn't or couldn't? It all went round and round in his head, holding sleep at arm's length and bringing his attention span down to negligible.

The morning of the day he felt comfortable returning to the studio – he was just going to casually pop in on his way back from work, and why not? – he woke with a soreness, just above the elbow of his right arm. He didn't think much of it and, as sleep slipped away from him he absently rubbed the area with his other hand. It was very sore. And slightly sticky. There was blood.

He looked down horrified to see the sheets that had been near his arm were also smeared with blood. Not a lot, but enough to be very shocking, but not as shocking as the shiny new tattoo that was under the crusted blood. And it was another tarot card. It was a similar style, but this one showed an individual behind a table or worktop, cluttered with mysterious paraphernalia and was titled "The Magician". The vine or creeper design behind the first card was here too and now joined up with the original Wheel of Fortune card. Small tendrils that had reached out from the original piece but terminated, now stretched and joined with those reaching out from The Magician with no trace of change or error, as if they had always been joined.

The Hanged Man

Marc phoned in sick that morning.

13

Death

"Dodgy guts? Something you ate?" said the voice at Marc's depot and he replied with some concoction about a kebab.

"Well, you can keep your squits to yourself, mate", continued the voice, "But it's a shame. I got an email from head office this morning, about you, and concerning a pay rise".

On his way out Marc noticed a letter from his employer that had dropped through the letterbox that morning. Opening and scanning it, it seemed he had indeed received a pay rise – something to do with rewarding him for 'Service Excellence', whatever that was. He slammed the half-read letter back onto the little table in the hallway and stormed out, heading straight for Danny's tattoo studio.

When he got there it was closed. It was difficult to tell, as the windows were blanked, hiding any lights that might be on, but on the door, between the glass and a roller blind a beautifully hand drawn sign, in traditional tattoo script and colours apologised and told him "Sorry, we're closed".

He tried the handle anyway. The door rattled, but was clearly locked. He stared at it for a moment, at a loss for what to do.

As he turned to leave, the side of the blind was pulled back and Sable looked out at him. He felt his blood run cold. He wanted to cheer and run away at the same time. He could feel his heart pounding in his chest. She didn't seem to have such a reaction but exaggeratedly mouthed the words "One moment", lifting her finger to signal him to wait, while she fiddled with the lock and eventually opened the door.

"Hello trouble!" she beamed as she got the door open, and threw her arms around his neck. Marc had absolutely no idea what to do.

"We're closed", she said. "But do you want to come in for a cuppa?"

Without waiting to see if he was following, which he naturally was, the young woman turned back into the studio's waiting area, leaving the door swinging open for Marc to close behind him. He watched her back as she disappeared through the

15

The Devil

plastic-strip curtain that separated the reception from the studio proper; her skin-tight black jeans curving up over her hips, shining black high heels stepping cat-walk style in front of each preceding step, the soft new-looking black t-shirt and her jet black hair with its scarlet streak bouncing on her shoulders.

"Kettle's not long boiled. Take a seat", she called over her shoulder and he did, on one of the little padded benches for waiting customers. He knew he had good reason to be there, but he felt foolish.

When she returned with two mugs of steaming tea, both vessels black, with the name of the tattoo and piercing studio curling across their surfaces in white, he lifted his sleeve and pointed at the new tarot tattoo.

"Look", was all he said.

Sable, meanwhile, gasped and bit her lower lip in pleasure and excitement.

"Oh my God!" she squealed. "He did it! It's going to work!"

Marc just looked at her, shook his head and shrugged questioningly.

"I told you he was, like, a wizard! You're going to have some more of those soon I reckon".

"What do you mean?" Marc really was nonplussed. He vaguely remembered some conversation in the club last weekend about magic, about gods from islands somewhere in the South Seas, who were responsible for painting all the fish in the ocean.

"The Magician! Ooooo!" Sable interrupted Marc's thoughts. "Have you had any good luck recently?"

"Well, I did just get a pay rise, but ..." he trailed off.

"You can expect a lot of that", grinned Sable, her unearthly eyes shining. "Who's a lucky boy?"

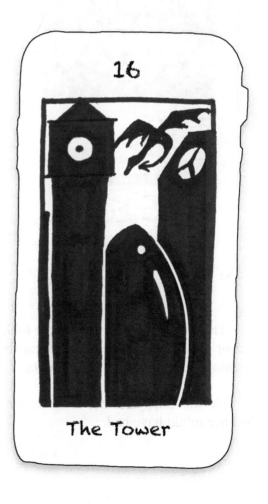

The Tower

17

The Star

She was standing very close to Marc now, where he was sitting on the little bench. He was confused and not a little worried, but he wanted to be with her so much.

He looked up at her delicate features with the fiendishly cute cleft in her chin. She put her hands on his shoulders. She now pressed herself against him.

"But … Danny?"

"Danny's not here right now".

A moment's pause.

"I think you'd better come with me" she said.

There was no argument, as she took Marc's hand, led him back out of the shop, closing and locking the door behind them, before opening the front door to her and Danny's flat and led him upstairs.

He was happy for her to be in control as he felt he'd lost any he once might have had.

* * *

Every few days, sometimes every couple of weeks, a new card would appear somewhere on his body. When it did Marc would go to the studio and every time he would find it shut up and locked. But when he knocked Sable was always there. And when Sable was always there Danny was always out.

When every new card appeared it wove itself into the growing web of the design, connecting all the Major Arcana – the picture cards of the tarot – into one, swarming, creeping deck of beautifully illustrated skin art. And with every new card there was something new in Marc's life. He had become famous among London's alternative set. People got to know about his new tattoos and would approach him and ask him if he'd had another new one done yet. The only time he saw Danny was one night in the Electric Ballroom, the same nightclub where he'd met him. Marc had just stripped off his top and was showing off the reticulated collage of cards that, by now, crawled up and down both arms, across his chest and down the tops of his thighs, leaving only his lower legs,

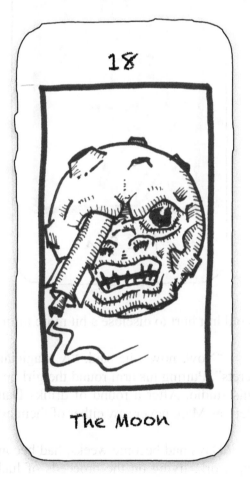

The Moon

19

The Sun

neck, head, face and back bare.

An attractive and clearly keen young cybergoth was cooing and stroking the cards one by one, asking question after question about their meanings, which Marc had been taking time to learn, and was fascinated about the process of having so much work done, and wanting to know the ins and outs of this growing piece of living art, when Danny appeared.

Smiling, but still giving off a powerfully commanding presence, Danny stepped up and cut in, when Marc had just decided that it couldn't hurt to disclose a bit more information to this girl.

"Now, now", he said. "A Magician never gives away his secrets". Putting his arm round the girl he interested her in a flyer for his studio. After a round of drinks Danny and the girl must have left, as Marc never saw either of them again that evening.

Days had become weeks, had become months. Marc had given up work, living on the proceeds of lucky bets he'd made. In fact when Marc decided to lay a bet he always seemed moved to know when and where to place it and never seemed to loose. He partied all night and slept all day, except when a new card showed itself and then he paid a visit to Sable who was always very pleased to see him.

His luck never seemed to falter; things couldn't be better. Enough money came in; when wanted a girl in a club he always seemed to pull her; when he'd bought a car he was rear-ended by someone whose insurance had paid enough to have that car customised – properly pimped. He moved into his own flat – a fabulous warehouse conversion at a knock down price. He'd even decided to go out some nights to places he didn't know he knew, and ended up having adventures where he met the rich and famous, including some of his rock idols. He even ran out of petrol near the house of a very famous front man from a heavy metal band that was still going from the early eighties and got invited in, to join the after show party that happened to be going on. He had, his friends said, the luck of the Devil, and life was sweet.

One morning, it must have been around a year after his first tattoo, Marc woke to find the final card had arrived.

In the centre of his back was card number thirteen: Death.

It was his original Grim Reaper tattoo: The scythe, rippling with fire, arcing over the snarling, hooded skull and spelling the words "You're mine", in perfectly spelled, perfectly calligraphed letters, exactly how he had imagined. In fact, it was better than he'd imagined. However he did it, this was a triumph of Danny's work.

Death, as Marc had learned many years ago, was not a card to be taken literally, but often interpreted as change: The end of one thing and the beginning of something new. There was nothing to worry about.

20

Judgement

He showered off the dried blood, dressed, applied some expensive aftershave he'd been given and went out for his usual visit to Sable, to show her the new and final card.

Smiling to himself and whistling, he fairly skipped down the road. How his life had changed. How much more rock-and-roll it was now than a year ago. He'd kept his head down, stayed true to the lifestyle and he'd received his reward.

What an amazing year it'd been.

When he reached the studio, which was closed, as it always was when he arrived, he gave a cheery rap on the glass and waited for the door to be opened. Sable peered round the blind as she always did, but Marc didn't notice that this time she had lost her girlish and rampant enthusiasm, and when she opened the door, she simply said, "You'd better come in".

And the door was closed and locked behind them.

* * *

Time passed and it took a while, three or four weeks, before people started wondering where Marc, or 'Tarot', as he'd become known, was. With no job to go to, no routine to observe, nobody regularly relying on seeing him, his absence had not been noticed.

In fact, having no reason to observe the conventions and regular activities of society his disappearance went almost completely unnoticed. People would occasionally ask, "Do you remember that guy who used to come in here – the one with all the tattoos?" But no one wondered where he went to now. He had simply ceased to 'pop up' in places where people only ever 'popped up'.

Eventually he became just a story that people reminisced about.

* * *

"And what about this fabulous piece?" asked the reporter.

Danny smiled as he turned to look at the stretched hide, framed and mounted on his studio wall. It was a masterpiece of his tattooing skill, showing all twenty two of the Tarot deck's main picture cards, from The Fool to The World, each woven together by intricate, curling and crossing vines. Laid out like this, it was quite large and must have taken months to complete.

"Pig skin", said Danny, linking his arm round Sable as she cuddled into his side.

"Long pig", added Danny, laughing at his own joke and waving away the reporter's confusion.

"This'll be a great double page spread for the article", said the reporter, lifting up her camera.

"Not this one", smiled Danny sadly, gently laying his hand on the lens. "Too many memories", he whispered.

"Anyway", he continued as the doorbell buzzed. "I've got some great works in progress to show you, that you can photograph for the mag. That must be them now – go and let them in, will you, love", he finished, giving Sable a squeeze.

"Great", the reporter smiled. "Is there nothing you can't do with some ink and a needle", grinned the reporter.

Danny laughed and shrugged with mock modesty.

Sable's strange eyes glistened and shone as she skipped off, yet again, to do as Danny asked.

21

The World

The Unluckiest Man on the Brass Coast

The Brass coast, as its name suggests, is a place where the land meets the sea.

With your back to the land, your eye will float over rolling waves of deep grey-blue to the horizon and beyond.

Turning now, to put the sea at your *back*, and looking over the land, again your eye floats over a sea of rolling waves that stretch to the horizon and beyond, but this time, the waves are great dunes of reddish-yellow sand that gives the nation its name.

But the Brass Coast is not entirely composed of barren desert. There are winding rivers and oases where subterranean water bubbles to the surface, and in these places the ground is fertile. Great palms sway, heavy with dates, wheat waves in the warm desert breezes, sheep and goats graze on juniper bushes and fish are drawn with lines or nets.

In one such place there lived a man: The Unluckiest Man on The Brass Coast.

At least, that is what he thought of himself and his life now, as he had not always been unlucky.

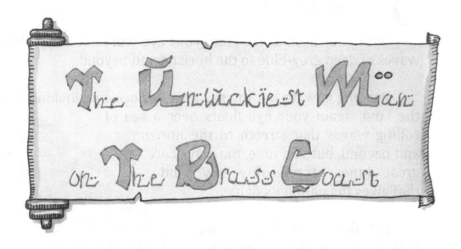

He had grown up on his parents' farm, not far from a great city, and with an orchard that grew, so his Father used to say, 'the most delicious peaches in the Empire'; but after his parents' deaths the farm hadn't worked the way it used to. Every year it seemed to grow fewer peaches and those peaches weren't quite as succulent or as sweet as the ones his Father had tended and he sold fewer and fewer every harvest.

An only child and unmarried, every night the Unluckiest Man on The Brass Coast would sit alone in the old farmhouse that had begun to tumble down. Day by day the curtains became more tattered, gaps appeared in the shutters, his clothes became more threadbare and the cloudless nights became colder and colder.

"Oh, woe is me", the Unluckiest Man on The Brass Coast would weep. "I am so unlucky that not even my house can keep me warm at night".

He burnt the table. He burnt the chairs. He burnt his bed and all the other things in the house that *would* burn until there was nothing left in the house *to* burn.

"I have nothing to sit on and nothing to sleep on. Surely I am the Unluckiest Man on The Brass Coast", he cried aloud to the world.

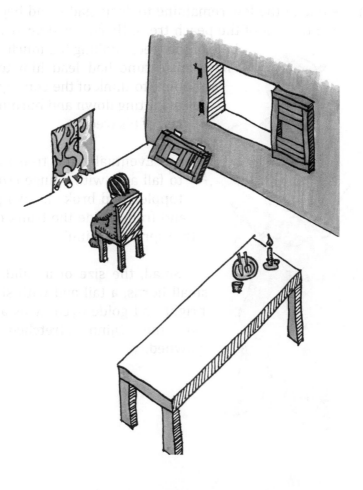

And so, one by one, he cut down the peach trees to use as firewood, and every night he would lie by the hearth in the ashes and the cinders, and think about how he was The Unluckiest Man on The Brass Coast.

Then, there came a day when he awoke to find there was only one peach tree remaining in what was once the orchard, but was now little more than dry, gritty sand, surrounded by a broken fence of splinters

Wearily, The Unluckiest Man on The Brass Coast took up his axe – one of the few remaining tools he had – and began to chop down the last of the peach trees. He chopped away at the bole of the tree, thinking too much about how misfortune had lead him to this sad point, to think of the consequences of cutting down and burning the last of his trees.

Eventually the tree started to fall and, with a huge *crack*! it toppled and broke in two parts, and from inside the trunk of the tree sprang a Djinn!

Small, the size of a child, with small horns, a tail and with skin as bright and golden-yellow as a lemon, the Djinn stretched and yawned.

"Thank you kindly, Farmer. I've been trapped inside that peach tree for nearly one hundred years. I am very lucky that you chose to chop it down".

"Then you are luckier than I", said The Unluckiest Man on the Brass Coast looking at the split tree trunk and the last three peaches that had rolled off the branches into the dust.

"Why are you so unlucky?" asked the Djinn, looking at the shabbily dressed man.

"Why, how could such bad fortune befall anyone who wasn't The Unluckiest Man on The Brass Coast?" he replied. "My parents are dead, I have no brothers or sisters, I have no wife and no children, my house is in tatters and my farm is reduced to firewood", he finished, pointing at the felled tree and the now dead orchard, filled only with dust and stumps.

"Well, today you are *not* The Unluckiest Man on The Brass Coast", said the Djinn, beaming and putting his hands on his hips. "As you have freed me from my imprisonment in that tree I will grant you three wishes".

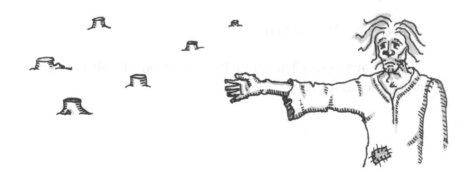

At this, The Unluckiest Man on The Brass Coast's eyes lit up and he looked up hopefully.

"But!" continued the Djinn suddenly, before the man could respond. "You must be careful what you wish for – luck can be capricious".

But the Unluckiest Man on The Brass coast wasn't listening. He'd heard the Djinn's promise of three wishes and knew what he needed to change his luck and make his life better.

"Think carefully for what you wish, before you wish your wish", said the Djinn with a wink and a grin.

But the Djinn's grin faded as the man ran headlong into wishing his first wish.

"I wish!" he blurted, a fire in his eyes. "I wish for as much gold as I can carry!"

The Djinn sat down sadly on the split trunk and shuffled his feet in the dust.

"Really?" he asked.

"Really", sad the man

"Sure?" the Djinn asked.

"Sure!" answered The Unluckiest Man on The Brass Coast, beaming and nodding.

"Very well", said the Djinn, and absently waved a hand in the air towards the man, making intricate and arcane shapes and gestures with his hand as he did so.

Suddenly, The Unluckiest Man on The Brass Coast felt his knees sag, as he was unexpectedly encumbered by a number of very heavy bags, filled with gold coins. Not too heavy, you understand, but just about as much as he could carry.

He was amazed. He hefted the bags, laughing and thanking the Djinn for changing his misfortune into fabulous riches.

"I will take this gold to the city, where I will use it to buy new clothes, with which to impress a potential wife, and buy new peach trees that will be more succulent and sweeter than the ones that failed me, and in my new clothes I shall visit the wizards and pay them to teach me great magic so that I can become The Most Powerful Man on The Brass Coast!"

The Djinn watched The Unluckiest Man on The Brass Coast as he shuffled off towards the city, staggering under the weight of the gold.

* * *

By the time The Unluckiest Man on the Brass Coast reached the city, the sun was beginning to set. Shadows stretched and there was a pause in the air, waiting for the night breezes to come and blow away the heat of the day.

It had taken some hours to reach the city walls as the man was staggering under the weight of the bags of gold that he had wished for, from the Djinn he'd freed. Of course, having wished for 'as much gold as I can carry', the man could indeed carry it, but only just.

Having passed through a gatehouse in the city walls, heavily tipping the guards with his new found wealth, he started to look around for an inn where he could spend the night before really enjoying his gold the next day, when the shops and stalls would be open again.

The streets he walked down grew quieter as he entered the city's unfamiliar depths. Turning into a particularly narrow alley, where a kind stranger had told him he might find an inn, he found his way blocked by a group of rough-looking individuals. They wore patched and ragged silks, their faces were scarred, teeth were missing and they carried a mixture of scimitars, knives and crude clubs. The man thought he could see the friendly stranger who had directed him amongst the group.

"Well, well, my friend", said the one who appeared to be their leader, with a gap-toothed grin. "What a heavy burden you seem to be carrying. Here; my friends and I will help you carry it".

"No. No, thank you", said The Unluckiest Man on The Brass Coast. "I can manage. It's just enough, so I can carry it and...". But his voice trailed away as the Leader stepped forward and brought the painfully sharp tip of his scimitar up under his chin.

"I said", the Leader growled. "My friends and I will carry it for you. *All* of it".

The man's shoulder's slumped and he let the bags of gold slide onto the floor with a solid *chink*.

"Now go! Run away and take your life, and be thankful you have that!" shouted the leader and the man scurried off.

Without a bean to his name, the man huddled with the beggars outside the city walls, telling himself over and over again, how he was, most definitely, 'The Unluckiest Man on The Brass Coast'.

* * *

In the morning he walked slowly back to what was left of his peach farm, his belly howling with hunger.

He found the Djinn sitting on the cracked trunk of the last peach tree, left where it had been felled. He saw the man's face and guessed that he'd lost all his money.

"I am simply The Unluckiest Man on the Brass Coast", said the man, slumping down next to the Djinn, his stomach growling.

"Well then, perhaps you'd like to think more carefully about your next wish", said the Djinn, offering the man one of his last three peaches, which he ate without even noticing.

"If only I had the power to change my luck", the man sighed sadly. "I know!" he cried suddenly, jumping up. "I will learn magic!"

"Do you know anything about magic?" asked the Djinn, a frown of concern wrinkling his normally smiling face.

"No, no, no ... but it doesn't matter does it? I've got wishes!"

"Oh yes", said the Djinn, starting to dread what was coming next.

"I wish I was full of magic! Yes! Full of it and buzzing with the power of magic!" he shouted.

"Very well. As you wish", said the Djinn moving his hands through the air and muttering strange words.

And suddenly, The Unluckiest Man on the Brass Coast was glowing, fizzing, buzzing with a mystical energy: Magical energy. He laughed, hopping and capering about, marvelling at the sparks and little stars that popped from his hair and fingertips.

"I shall now go to the Tower of Magic in the city and I shall show those wizards that they should welcome me in, as I am powerful!"

And off he strode, back to the city.

"*Full of power*, yes, but not necessarily *powerful*", mumbled the Djinn, shaking his head and watching the receding back of the man.

* * *

The Tower of Magic was an impressive building.

Great flat stones paved a wide square around the Tower, meaning anyone approaching the great door felt very exposed and vulnerable. The Tower itself was made of immense blocks of stone, far too large for any human ingenuity to lift by hand or crane. Legend said that the huge edifice had been drawn out of the earth and molded by the hands of great elemental beings of rock and stone, called by the wizards who had first inhabited it, hundreds and hundreds of years ago. The arched windows that pierced the outer wall at irregular intervals gave the impression of many eyes that peered and watched.

Nothing grew or moved between the outer perimeter and the Tower so, even feeling the warm buzz of pure Magic vibrating through his body, it was an intimidating walk for the man, as he approached the great tower.

He began to question the wisdom of his second wish and kept looking up at the windows and over his shoulder, feeling that he was being followed or escorted by unseen servants.

The entrance to the tower had been fashioned to look like a great face, with huge double doors making the mouth. The eyes of this statuesque mask seemed to follow the man as he approached, making him feel as if that mouth might suddenly lunge forward and engulf him.

Caught in his fantasy and before he had a chance to knock on the great doors, they opened inwards and a tall wizard stood between them in the opening, staring imperiously down at him.

"What do you want?" demanded the sorcerer.

The Unluckiest Man on the Brass Coast could feel the Magic coursing through him and took courage, "I am a great and powerful wizard and I have come to be recognised by you and the other wizards of this Tower for my great power!"

"Really?" sneered the wizard. "You look more like a beggar".

"How DARE you!" shouted the man feeling the Magic bubble and surge through him such that even the wizard took a step back.

"Do you know the secrets of alchemy?" the wizard asked, now interested, but the man shook his head.

"Can you command a ritual?"

Again, no.

"Do you know the great grimoires?"

"Can you summon elementals?"

"Are you a member of a school of magic?"

And each time, no.

"You don't know anything of magic, but yet you seem to have power", said the wizard eventually.

"Yes", replied the man. "I have been granted power and I am full of magic", he continued, remembering his words and starting to feel things might slip way from him again.

The wizard moved his staff through the air and spoke a few, short, alien-sounding words and The Unluckiest Man on The Brass Coast began to glow and the wizard's eyes opened wide with greater interest.

Before he could get over his surprise, the wizard smartly rapped him on the forehead, and the fizzing, buzzing magic flowed out of his body and into the staff, making the wizard beam.

"There. That's that fixed and thank you for your gift of power. Now go away and don't meddle in things you clearly have no understanding of", said the wizard, and slammed the door in the man's face.

He knew the magic had gone. He knew that his second wish and been spent and nothing had come of it. With a heavy heart, he turned and walked away from the Tower of Magic and left the city, heading back to his ramshackle home.

* * *

His third and final wish went just as badly.

He wished for the most beautiful wife in the world, but by the day she had appeared – and it was a miserable day for both of them, arguing in his empty, cold and crumbling house – she left, and returned to the man she was *already* married to, she being the most beautiful wife in the world, but sadly already the wife of *another* man.

So, sadly and, again bemoaning the fact he was The Unluckiest Man on The Brass Coast, he sat on the ground in the shade of his house.

* * *

Presently, the Djinn walked over and handed the man the last two peaches from the last, lost peach tree, "You have had three wishes – riches, magical power and greatest of beauties – but they have brought you only misery and emptiness. Now here are the last two peaches from your Father's peach farm that brought him so much happiness".

But the man didn't seem to listen and just bit into one of the peaches.

It was delicious.

It was the most delicious thing he had tasted.

IT WAS So...
DĔLICIOUS

He had forgotten how the peaches from his family farm were the most delicious peaches in the land, and before he realised he'd eaten the entire fruit!

His hunger sated for the moment, he looked at the other, last peach.

"You know", he started. "I think I could sell this and make a little money".

The Djinn said nothing, but quietly looked around at the rough stumps of what was once a blossoming and productive orchard.

"Right!" said The Unluckiest Man on The Brass Coast standing up, full of decision and resolve, and he took the remaining peach and returned to the city, where he marched up to the palace and got directions to the kitchens.

At the kitchen door, the palace's chief cook began to turn The Unluckiest Man on The Brass Coast away, waving a cleaver menacingly at him, until he saw the peach that the man was trying to sell.

The chief cook was overjoyed! The Grand Vizier – the Royal adviser – had just been berating him for not having any peaches for the Royal Supper and now, here was a peach he needed. He gingerly took the fruit from The Unluckiest Man on The Brass Coast's in his vast, pudgy hand, being careful not to bruise its flesh.

"Stay here!" he said, dragging the man in, through the door. "I'll be back shortly – either with the High Executioner, or a reward of gold for you, beggar man, depending on whether His Majesty enjoys this peach or not".

Turning on his heel, the chief cook wobbled off to wash and slice the peach for *the Royal Supper*, leaving The Unluckiest Man on The Brass Coast under the watchful eye of a number of kitchen hands, all with cleavers and knives of bewildering variety, and sure that his bad luck would mean his imminent execution.

Time passed slowly in the hot kitchen where steam made a man sweat his worth, and smoke carried the sting of chilies into the eyes and lungs, but eventually the chief cook returned, grinning and swaggering and tossing a small purse of coins in one hand.

"You're in luck", he said, planting a heavy, meaty paw on The Unluckiest Man on The Brass Coast's shoulder. "His Majesty said it was the most delicious peach he'd ever tasted. The Grand Vizier has instructed me to say that I can buy all the peaches from you that you can supply", and grinning, pressed the small moneybag onto the man's chest.

Now, being The Unluckiest Man on The Brass Coast, instead of being pleased to be paid for his last peach, he thought only of the lost orchard and how misfortune had forced him to chop down all the trees, leaving him with nothing. He thanked the chief cook but shuffled back out of the palace and into the streets.

The day was coming to its end in the city streets, and The Unluckiest Man on The Brass Coast watched the stallholders packing away they wares: The draper with silks and cloths that would have made a fine wedding gown, if he'd had a wife, and the jewelers with their gold and silver and sparkling stones that would have made people understand just how rich he was, if he'd had any wealth. Lastly there was a stall run by an old wizard. You could tell the man was a wizard by his voluminous clothes, printed and embroidered with mystical signs, sigils and symbols, but it was difficult to tell what he was selling as the scrolls and bottles and bundles were far too arcane to be easily recognisable. His curiosity peaked, The Unluckiest Man on The Brass Coast wandered over to get a closer look.

As he approached the old wizard peered up at him, from under his big, bushy white eyebrows.

"You don't' look like someone who can afford my special things?" he asked.

"Oh, I'm just looking, thank you", started the Man. "But I do have money. Well – I have money today", he finished, lifting up the small bag of coins.

"'Money today' is the best kind of money", smiled the wizard. "Now, what can I show you?"

"Oh, nothing, thank you", said the man, his face falling. "With my luck you won't have anything to help me".

"Help is it, you need? What sort of help?" asked the wizard, warming to his customer.

"What I really need is to be able to grow peaches, like the ones that grew in my Father's orchard, but I need them to grow overnight, and I doubt such a thing exists to make that happen".

But the old wizard's eyes widened and he started to rummage in the sandalwood chests and heavily woven carpetbags he'd been packing.

"Do you have a pit?" called the old wizard over his shoulder.

"A what?" replied the man, confused.

"A pit – a stone, the seed that is the rock-hard centre of one of the peaches?"

The Unluckiest Man on The Brass Coast thought and yes, he probably did. The one from the peach he'd eaten earlier must be lying in the dust near the chopped down peach tree and the Djinn.

"Yes. Yes, I think I have", answered the man, beginning to feel some of the old wizard's enthusiasm.

"Ah-ha!" cried the magician from the depths of a bag, woven from thick scarlet, black and blue wool. He stood up and in his jeweled and ringed fingers he held out a small, stoppered bottle, no longer than the middle bone of a man's finger.

"This!" he pronounced. "Is the last bottle of its kind ... in the world!"

The man was intrigued.

"I bought this from an alchemist, who came from a country where it rains every fourth day, and the fields and hills and mountains are green all year. A few drops of this will make a plant grow overnight! If you were to plant the stone of your peach and add a few drops of this directly onto it, by morning you'll have fresh, ripe peaches", grinned the wizard.

The Unluckiest Man on The Brass Coast was overjoyed.

"How much do you want for it?" he asked, eagerly opening the strings on the little moneybag. Both the man and the old wizard were disappointed by what was inside. It was, however, as the wizard had said 'money today'.

"I'll tell you what I'll do", said the old wizard. "It's the end of the day and you look like you could use some help. I'll let you have the potion for the coins you have there but you bring me a peach in the morning and we'll call it an even bargain".

"Thank you! Thank you! I will," cried The Unluckiest Man on The Brass Coast, taking the little potion bottle and running off, towards the city gates and his home.

Almost without stopping, racing the sunset, The Unluckiest Man on The Brass Coast arrived back at his dusty barren farm and just about managed to choke out enough words to the Djinn, who handed him the last peach pit from his Father's orchard.

Hurriedly, with a piece of broken fence post that had yet to be burned, The Unluckiest Man on The Brass Coast scraped away enough of the dusty earth to form a hollow, into which he dropped the peach stone. Next, he uncorked the potion bottle and tapped out a few drops of iridescent green liquid onto the nut-like seed, before covering it up again and gently patting the ground flat.

The man then excitedly bade the Djinn goodnight, before curling up on the hard floor next to the cold ashes in the fireplace, and slept a fitful sleep, with beautiful dreams of lands where thick forests of giant peach trees spread to the horizon, waving in cool breezes, and warm, gentle waters dropped from the skies into sapphire pools, bounded by lawns that were cropped by fat sheet and goats, and as luxuriously thick as a nomad's green felt carpet.

In the morning he woke from his idyllic dreaming to feel a familiar dread sink from his stomach to his unshod feet. What if the potion hadn't worked? That would be typical of his bad luck. What if the potion was a fake! That would be even more like his bad luck!

Wearily he dragged himself to his feet, dusted down his now ragged clothing and walked to the open doorway of the farmhouse and looked out.

Against all odds and ignoring the fact that this man was The Unluckiest Man on The Brass Coast, on the spot where he had planted the peach stone the evening before, there was now a fully mature peach tree, its branches weighed heavy with ripe peaches. At its base, the little, golden skinned Djinn reclined with his back against the trunk, complimenting the man on the sweet, succulent and delicious flesh of the peach he was eating, and enjoying watching the look of amazement spreading across his face.

The Unluckiest Man on The Brass Coast couldn't believe his luck – it had worked! As quickly as he could, stopping only to briefly breakfast on one of the miraculous peaches, he used his shirt to bundle up as many fruits as he could carry and hurried off to the city and the palace.

The Unluckiest Man on The Brass Coast was a sorry sight at the door to the kitchens, dressed only in patched and thread-bare trousers.

His last shirt, covered in dust, earth and soaked in peach juice was in one hand, but in the other was a bag of money –

significantly larger than the one he'd received yesterday. Smiling and relaxed for the first time in a long time, he remembered the old wizard's request for a peach and trotted over to where the stalls were now all laid out for a day's noisy and colourful trading. But the stallholders didn't recognise the description of the old wizard or his stall.

Confused, but happy with his earnings, The Unluckiest Man on The Brass Coast used some of his money to buy a new bed and some equipment for fixing up his house and farm and even rented a camel to take it all back with him.

He worked hard all that day, making repairs and clearing the land where the old orchard had stood, and planted more peach stones and anointed them with the remaining doses from the potion bottle, before taking the camel back the next morning to the city, laden with peaches – some of which he sold at a very high price to the palace kitchens and some he sold at the market.

This time, with his earnings, he bought some fine new clothes and furnishings for his house.

As the days passed, he became quite the merchant in the city, investing his money in other areas of business, whilst tending to his new orchard, now having a fine collection of mature, fruiting trees, using up the last of the potion.

It was a few days time later that he realised he hadn't seen the Djinn for some time and that he must have moved on, back to wherever Djinns go in the desert wastes.

The peaches from the newly grown trees continued to please all who ate them, and being a peach farmer was good for the man.

In time, he met a beautiful and clever woman whom he courted and eventually married, and they had a wonderful collection of sons and daughters. Together they grew the farm and their property and their businesses, and long before his eldest son inherited the farm, The Unluckiest Man on The Brass Coast came to think of himself instead, as The Luckiest Man on the Brass Coast.

With his children and, later, his grandchildren, the man would sit them on a particular bench carved from half of a split peach tree and tell them the story of how he once thought of himself as unlucky and how the very bench they were sitting on was made from a tree which he had once felled and had contained a Djinn, trapped for one hundred years.

They loved his stories and asked for them over and over again, but none of them really believed that the Djinn was real, nor had there been an old wizard with a potion who had then vanished, and that these mature peach trees could be nothing other than the orchard that the man himself had inherited from his father and, while he had grieved hard when his parents had gone and sought help in his loneliness, these were all just fables, told to entertain and to teach them to be good people when they grew up.

Maybe his children were right that these were just stories.

Maybe they weren't.

But what the Luckiest Man on The Brass Coast's stories taught them was that while fortune and misfortune may sometimes pull this way or that at the reins of life, in the end we make our own luck, and with wit, hard work and faith, we can achieve more than we ever thought we could.

Dream Eater

On the eastern coast of one of the smaller Japanese islands there is a fishing village. Akiko had moved there to live with her Grandfather, when she was nine, after her Father had died.

She *had* lived in a big city where great steam engines brought food, by rail, from towns and villages far away and she'd loved to spend time watching the gleaming locomotives puff and chuff their ways into the busy station on shining rails, where important men swaggered in their western suits, soldiers walked stiffly in their smart uniforms and beautiful, glamorous ladies wrapped in their kimonos and obis and with painted faces, tiptoed past on wooden sandals, talking and giggling modestly behind their fans.

Her Father had worked on the railways as a goods manager, a job to be proud of, especially with his humble beginnings as a fisherman's son, but it was also his downfall when, one day, he'd got caught between shunting trucks and later died at home in his wife's arms, watched by his little daughter.

Not long after that awful day Akiko and her mother moved to live with her Grandfather – her Father's Father – in a small house that was built partly on the land and partly on stilts out over the sea, in a sheltered bay with black rocks and deep water.

She loved her Grandfather and he was always kind to her even though, since her Father's death, and too old to fish anymore, he had become very quiet and prone to spending time looking out to sea, and painting pictures that he never showed anyone, and always threw away. She loved her Grandfather, but his house was dark, had waves, lapping under her bedroom at high tide, made strange noises at night, and had a feeling of loneliness and that there were people missing who should have been there.

Akiko spent her days going to school and learning to like the new children she met, who knew nothing about trains and big cities, but told her about the sea and the rocks and weather and the sky.

At night she didn't dream.

She'd not dreamt since her Father had died.

She would lie awake listening to the quiet noises of the fishing village, of the waves against the piles supporting the portion of the building over the water, and the strange noises in that dark and lonely house until she found herself waking to the morning and her Mother rousing her for school or chores around their new home.

She hadn't dreamt since her Father had died.

She hadn't dreamt until the Umibōzu came.

The children at the village school had told her about the Umibōzu and how it came from the cold, dark places under the sea – the place where lost souls went – and she had told them how silly they were and how such things couldn't possibly exist in a world of steam locomotives and cannons and factories.

But it didn't stop the Umibōzu from coming.

The first night it came to visit Akiko she had felt she was lying awake in her darkened bedroom. A high tide was nuzzling the house underneath her and a ragged moon made shadow puppets from her curtains when she first heard the creak of oars in their locks.

Even before the shadow of the Umibōzu blotted out the moon-lit window she knew what it was that approached her quiet, lonely room, from the quiet, lonely parts of the coal-black sea.

She became rigid with fear when she heard and felt the boat bump into one of the wooden supports outside. Unable to cry out and paralyzed by the dream, she watched as the silhouetted figure of a man climbed up the outside of her bedroom wall. His head was large and round and appeared to be clean-shaven, like a priest, while his body moved and shifted with a ghost-like insubstantiality and his arms coiled and writhed like snakes, or an octopus's tentacles.

Akiko could do nothing, as the Umibōzu opened her window and part slid, part drifted and part climbed in to lean over her, in her bed. And then she woke, shaking and crying, alone in the dark.

That was the first night little Akiko had the dream.

And then the dreams continued.

The dreams were always about the Umibōzu. It would row its boat from the far reaches of the wild and deep ocean to her window, where it would climb in and leer over her and tell her stories of the horrors of the deep. It would tell her how it had sunk a ship, or dragged a crew into the cold dark, how it would watch the souls of those who were lost wander the soundless fathoms where great whales dove and battled with squid as large as the locomotives she'd loved. And each time Akiko, thinking herself awake, would suddenly wake for real in the dark of her room, her face chilled with her own tears.

One morning, after a particularly stormy night, her Grandfather had remarked that a barrel had gone missing from outside their house and must have been swept into the sea. But Akiko knew what had really happened as, just like the legends said, when the Umibōzu had visited her the night before it had told her it had come for a barrel, to fill with sea water in which to drown sailors. This must have been the barrel it had taken.

Now, Akiko was only nine, and she had already known tragedy in her short life, but sadness is the other side of the coin of happiness and she knew she had to beat the demons in her dreams in order to be free of them, so she quietly asked advice of her Grandfather who was very old and, therefore, naturally very wise.

She asked him how – just for the sake of conversation, you understand – how one might go about beating a demon or something that haunted the night … if such a thing might ever occur to someone … else.

Her Grandfather looked directly at her, into her eyes and into her soul and his weather-browned face wrinkled in a sad smile.

He told her that such a person might make an offering at a shrine, such as the old, ruined one she passed on her way to school, and that an offering should be to that person's ancestors and to the gods and be made from good food, set aside for the occasion.

She thanked him and didn't realise, the next morning, that her Grandfather had encouraged her Mother to pack too much lunch for Akiko's school day and to separate the food for his Granddaughter's lunch from another parcel of food, neatly and carefully wrapped.

On her way to school, Akiko took the opportunity to use this extra food as an offering at the old Shinto shrine and did her best to be solemn and pray to her ancestors – even if she wasn't quite sure who they were – and to the gods, for help to banish the Umibōzu.

Night came and found Akiko lying scared and alone in her bed, listening to the waves, listening for the sound of the creaking of oars.

But this night things were different.

Instead of being alerted by the sound of an approaching boat, Akiko found herself sitting bolt upright as the room was filled with a bright silver glow from the full moon. She was afraid – or rather, in awe – as suddenly stepping in through her bedroom door was a figure in full battle armour.

There were flat shoulder plates made from strips of metal, knotted with scarlet lacing and a breastplate with the intricate design of a chrysanthemum embossed on it. The left hand whose back was shielded by a plate of molded, hammered steel rested, fingers curling around a sword's handle, bound with criss-cross fabric, sheathed and thrust through the binding belts at the warrior's waist. Under the other arm was a helmet with a sweeping back, formed from interlocking plates and strips, to protect the neck when worn, and completed with a faceplate of bronze: a grotesque grimace, snarling out at the world.

But the most remarkable thing about the proud and clearly capable, seasoned warrior that stood in Akiko's room that night was that the owner of the armour was not a man but a woman: an onna-bugeisha, a female samurai.

A beautiful woman's face smiled calmly and kindly down at the little girl in her bed. She told Akiko that she was her Grandmother of many generations before, who had had to take up arms when there were no longer any men to fight. She told her how she had come from Heaven and that Akiko's prayers had been heard and that she knew of the Umibōzu's nightmare visits and how her Granddaughter of many generations hence had asked for help.

Akiko's cheek's burned with embarrassment, but her Grandmother of many generations past furrowed her brow and admonished the girl, saying that without fear there can be no true bravery.

She then told her that while she could not help her directly, as her visit tonight was all that Heaven would allow, Akiko could help herself by calling on the help of the Dream Eater.

The Baku, she explained, was a magical animal, with the body of a pig, the feet of a tiger, the tail of an ox, the nose of an elephant, and the eyes of a rhinoceros.

She told Akiko that she must draw a picture of the Baku before going to bed and, if the Umibōzu should visit her in her nightmares she should say the words, "Baku-san, come eat my dreams. Baku-san, come eat my dreams. Baku-san, come eat my dreams".

Having delivered her message and smiling kindly at the child, the onna-bugeisha, Akiko's Grandmother of many generations past, pulled on her helm with its snarling faceplate and pulled the thongings tight under her chin. Then, in one swift movement her right hand swept onto the sword handle and without stopping drew the silver blade which sang from its sheath and cut an arc through the night air, splitting the darkness and allowing the golden morning sun to pour through the bedroom window, waking Akiko to a fresh and hopeful morning.

* * *

That night, after acquiring some paper and charcoal from her Grandfather, she drew a picture; a picture of this curious chimera, with the body of a pig, the feet of a tiger, the tail of an ox, the nose of an elephant and the eyes of a rhinoceros, before settling down to sleep.

In the dark and slumbering hours, from the depths of the sea the Umibōzu came that night.

The bump of its boat outside sent Akiko's heart racing and her eyes opened wide with fear, her breathing quickened as its shadow crept across the window.

Then it came in, its great bald head shining, its arms twisting jointlessly, whispering secrets of the lost deeps, of bones and tears and places where jawless eels creep in the lightless cold, looking for salt-tendered flesh on which to feast whilst decades passed.

But Akiko, remembering the words of her ancestor, summoned up her courage through the shallows of her fears, and cried out the words, "Baku-san! Come eat my dreams! Baku-san! Come eat my dreams! Baku-san! Come eat my dreams!"

The Umibōzu stopped in the middle of its tales of terror and looked to a dark corner of the room, and in that darkness two, yet darker, eyes blinked back.

Stepping from the shadow came a curious beast made, as if from several others: It had the body of a pig, the feet of a tiger, the tail of an ox, the nose of an elephant and the eyes of a rhinoceros.

The Umibōzu's face contorted in fury at the appearance of the Baku and its rage brought the storms and the winds and waves beat against the walls of Akiko's bedroom and spilled in, through the window, filling her room with seawater.

But the Baku, after casting a glance at the Umibōzu simply dipped its trunk-like nose into the salt water and sucked, and sucked until all the water had vanished.

This only served to enrage the Umibōzu yet further and as its fury increased, so did the fury of the storm. Akiko, trapped between the hideous Umibōzu and the stoic but fantastical-looking Baku watched, unable to cry out or run.

Then, like a painted piece of paper on the wall being grasped in its centre by someone with wetted fingertips, the Baku sucked at the Umibōzu and the window and storm, and whole of the nightmare crumpled and folded, was stretched and dragged, screaming in anger, into the Baku's snout with a noise like water rushing down a lead pipe, until suddenly … there was silence.

The Umibōzu had gone, the storm had gone, and all was quiet in Akiko's room. The only noises she could hear were the faint sounds of the fishing village and the waves lapping against the wooden stanchions. The Baku, on its short, strong legs walked over to Akiko and lay down beside her, like a large and comforting guard dog and stayed until Akiko's dream slipped away entirely.

In the morning there was, of course, no trace of the Baku and also no trace of seawater in her room and no rowing boat moored up outside her window.

From that night on, Akiko began to dream again. Most of the time they were dreams that didn't bother her and were the usual jumbled compendium of surreal moments where she was receiving presents, playing with kittens, helping her Grandfather or her Mother, or other mundane day-to-day events. But on some nights she, like all of us, still had the occasional nightmare. And on those nights she would cry, "Baku-san, come eat my dream! Baku-san, come eat my dream! Baku-san, come eat my dream!" and, from a shadow within a shadow, the Baku would come and gobble up whatever horrors had come to visit, and then keep her safe until morning.

Swipe Right

She stood, looking out of the window.

The window stretched from floor to ceiling and, in turn, stood on the side of a tower of glass and steel; offices at its base, exclusive and *very* private flats towards the top.

She watched the red eye of the sun, closing on the western horizon. She liked to watch the sun go down. She also liked to watch the sun rise. She spent a lot of time looking out of the window – looking for the sign. She knew that *when* the sign came it would be just as visible in the day but, irrational as she knew it was, she was always more hopeful that the sign would come at night.

Earlier in the evening she'd gone to the wardrobes that covered an entire wall of the apartment. Her feet stepped across rugs, made from the skins of long-dead animals, exotic in their antiquity. The rest of the rooms – as many and as spacious in this high-rise city penthouse as a large suburban dwelling – were sparsely but luxuriously decorated: Great, gilt-edged mirrors, their glass mottled and flowed with age, their baroque frames heavy, curlicued and gleaming; tables with thick, black, marble tops; chairs and sofas from all corners of the world, and cabinets containing artifacts so old and so rare that there was little chance or point in putting a price on them, so singular was their provenance.

She had opened the wardrobe doors, letting them concertina, folding back, one upon the next, upon the next, to reveal her outfits. She'd sighed at some of the more tired ones that were, by now, eons old, and selected something more modern to put on.

She'd dressed, made herself look nice and taken a selfie with her phone.

Then she'd uploaded it, named this city as her location, picked a name for herself, lied about her age, left most of the other details blank, published the profile and went back to the window to watch and to wait.

Less than an hour later she had arranged a date with a stranger, and went out to meet the man in the depths of the city.

They'd met, they had talked, *he* had drunk, and later that evening, she'd returned home with the man.

He had told her how beautiful she was, how sexy she was. *He* had told her exactly what he was thinking and exactly what *he* wanted.

She had looked into his eyes and into his heart and into his soul and seen darkness there.

She had met many men – and women – this way and all were sinners, but some were in need of more immediate judgment from a higher power and so, by way of atonement for her own sins, she would send them on their way to be judged and punished or forgiven, as her Father saw fit.

She felt the man's pulse and breathing quicken as he took a step towards her. She'd been very careful about what she'd said, not leading him on – not entrapping him – he'd come here of his own accord, of his own free will. He put his hand under her chin, lifting up her face and looking into her tear-filled eyes, and this made him smile even more.

She looked back, into his eyes, observing their colour and noticing how the pupils dilated with his excitement and anticipation.

And then she truly opened her eyes, and a light so bright it burned with white fire shone out, and as she looked into the man's eyes, she looked into his heart and into his soul and looked at what lay hiding there.

Without a cry, without a sound and without a struggle, the man's eyes widened, his mouth opened, as if in amazement, and then he slowly crumpled in her arms and a long breath sighed from him.

Once she was sure that he had gone – truly gone – she let his body gently down onto the expensively tiled and easily cleaned floor, before going to a cabinet and retrieving a knife so finely crafted that nothing on Earth could match its sharpness and balance, and that had been forged long before humans had raised themselves up off their knuckles.

And then, with that knife, she went to work.

* * *

Later she opened the wardrobe doors again and this time carefully hung up the new outfit, before tossing in a handful of mothballs towards the far end. She then slid off the outfit she was wearing and returned that to its place.

Now, just a creature of bone, as black as can only be blackened by the charring of divine fire, it closed the wardrobe doors.

Hips and shoulders wide enough to be strong, but not wide enough to be masculine or feminine, on its back two jointed bones that no human carried flexed and waved, severed to stumps with a blade that only divine power could sharpen to such keen-ness, and wielded against it, when it and the others fell.

Now, it stood once more at the window, overlooking the nighted city, but staring up into the star-filled firmament, looking for a sign that its offering would appease its Father and that it would once more be welcomed Above and no longer be consigned to suffer, here, Below, forever in search of others' sin with which to wash itself clean.

The Onion Man

If you don't know what a tabla is, it is a drum. They are usually played in pairs, one larger and shaped like a metal gourd about the size of a man's head, and the other, smaller one, an upright cylinder. They sit on cloth pads on the floor in front of the tabla player, who is also seated on the floor, and who plays one with each hand. They are small, as drums go, especially when compared to the European timpani – the kettle drum – or some of the larger Japanese taiko drums, but they are extraordinary in their ability to produce a number of different sounds and timbres, depending on where the drummer strikes them and with what part of their hand; sometimes with deft, single percussive blows and at other times a flurry of staccato fingertip pitter-pats. Some of the noises are light and dry like a bird pecking a tree, while others are low and bounce, like a pebble dropped into a deep well.

This story is about a man who played the tabla, and a very good tabla player he was too. But that was not the most interesting, nor, by far, the most extraordinary thing about him.

* * *

Many years ago in India, a long time before the British came, when Maharajas ruled their kingdoms, where proud, swaggering Rajput warriors kept bandits and invaders at bay with their long, blunt-nosed swords and three-bladed daggers, and peacocks drifted and cried on the lawns of watered gardens, there lived a man.

Not only was he a tabla player, but he also had an extraordinary magic gift.

Well, some would call it a gift, but some others called it a curse as it brought him fortune and misfortune in equal parts: He had the ability to change his shape and his appearance.

When he took off a set of clothes, if he wished he could cast them aside and they would turn to dust and be blown away on the wind, and he then had the appearance of someone else entirely. His face, his height, his build, his new clothes – everything about him had completely changed. His ability to shed layers and reveal a new person beneath lead to him becoming known as the Onion Man.

Sometimes he would do this for the entertainment of others, but the people in the village he lived in started to wonder if he would change his shape to deceive them. Sometimes, when someone was accused of theft or brawling or any other of a number of crimes, they would offer the defence that it was not they who had done this thing, but it must have been the Onion Man, disguised as them.

Eventually, the jealousies, the accusations and the mistrust meant that the Onion Man couldn't stay in the village he had been born in, and so decided to leave.

He took his tablas and headed to the city of the Maharaja's palace, where no one would know him and he could start again and earn a living just as a musician.

But life in the city was much harder than he expected. The people weren't any nicer than his old village. No one had any time nor the opportunity to give him, a mere musician, a chance or employment as a musician.

So, without regular work or a group of other musicians to play with, he took to busking in the streets. At night he would hide in the shadows and sleep alongside the other beggars, and in the morning he would wake, rise, strip off his dirty clothes and cast them to the wind, where they would turn to dust and float away. He would then return to what had become his regular spot on a busy street, now dressed in bright and colourful clothing, which made people feel more generous towards him than the dirty and ragged beggars. And so he scraped a living, playing tabla for the world as it walked by him.

* * *

It will come as no surprise to say that, after some while, the Onion Man tired of playing in the hot, dusty and dirty streets and wished for more from his life.

As he would sit on the ground, playing his tablas and thanking people for the coins they tossed to him he would look up at the high city walls, where monkeys from the nearby forest would jump and run and play.

How he envied their agility, their freedom, and wished he could be like a monkey with no responsibilities, able to go where he liked and be whoever he wanted.

At the start of the next morning, instead of going to his usual spot to play his tablas, he walked out of the city gates and around the high walls, with their carved and decoratively pierced stone crenulations, to where the monkeys came out of the forest and to the city.

He saw the monkeys, already high up on the city walls, having climbed the creepers or used the cracks and gaps between the stone blocks to gain purchase, and here he cast away his tablas, leaving them at the base of the walls as a gesture of renouncing his old life.

Checking no one could see him, he pulled off his clothes and threw them aside, and they turned to dust and blew away. As he threw away the clothes he was dressed, in what remained was not a naked man … but a monkey.

Finally he felt free and ran, bursting with joy and excitement, on all fours, to the base of the wall, where he climbed the creepers and the stone blocks until he too reached the top of the city wall.

From up here, it seemed like all of life was set out below him in the city. He could see the market, the palace, the temples, the shops and houses, even the street where he had played his tablas. Now he felt like a king – like the Maharaja himself – surveying his land and his subjects, with no one to bother or accuse him.

Or so he thought.

What the Onion Man didn't realise was, being a monkey had its own set of rules. The troupe had its hierarchies and roles, and strangers were not welcome.

Greeting the other monkeys as they approached him, the Onion Man was shocked when a big male suddenly snarled and barked, rolling his top lip back to show bright pink gums, and fearsomely long and dangerously pointed canine teeth. Another and then another joined in, making clear their threats, some feinting charges at him, until he took to his four heels and ran, the rest of the troupe chasing him, seeing him off, shrieking and barking at him until he'd reached an acceptable distance away, now in a different part of the city.

The Onion Man was crestfallen and depressed. Yes, he was agile and could run and jump and leap around, but he was, yet again, lonely and an outcast.

He also realised he was hungry.

Now he had no coins to spend and no way to communicate even if he had, so he decided to use his new agility to take whatever food he could from the market, just like the other monkeys did.

Nimbly he climbed down the city wall and bounded across the rooftops to the market. He scampered down the side of the building he was on, trotted over to the nearest stall and, while the man was busy serving a customer, helped himself to some delicious, ripe fruit.

Of course, as soon as the man noticed he ran, shouting and waving at the Onion Man in his monkey form, picking up a stick and swinging it wildly to chase him away.

This happened a few more times, with the Onion Man filling his belly, whilst dodging – not always successfully – the furious blows of the stallholders.

Full, but bruised, tired and lonely, at the end of the day, the Onion Man found a tiny, deserted observation tower on the city walls where he curled up and spent the night.

* * *

In the morning, after a bit of fruit theft, this time with fewer bruises, and having been chased off again by the city's resident monkey troupe, the Onion Man climbed the city walls and gazed out over the forest and the grassy plains, deep in introspection.

The sun rose higher, making the plains and top of the forest shimmer in the heat. In the distance, high in the blue and cloudless sky, he could see vultures, circling on the rising currents of hot air.

They looked so peaceful and tranquil, simply drifting, hanging on the wind, weaving in and out of each other; not interfering, not squabbling, not judging, just ... being.

How nice it would be to be a bird, to be one of the vultures and just glide on the thermals. In fact it was so enticing, the Onion Man pulled at the monkey skin on his chest and it came away, like a shirt, bringing the rest of the monkey skin with it and, with a flick, tossed its disintegrating folds onto the winds.

Underneath the monkey skin, the Onion Man had become a majestic vulture: Large, heavy body, an imperious head on a serpentine neck and with a curved blade of a beak, thick, scaly legs with strong claws. But it was the wings that were the most impressive part of his new body. He stretched them out, spanning a width greater than height of the tallest of men and tipped with finger-like feathers ... and he leapt into space.

There was a moment of uncertainty and then he felt the wind push up under his wings and his tail and he beat the air strongly, relishing the feeling of power as he climbed higher into the sky.

Up and up he went until something in him felt that this was the right place and the right time, and the Onion Man stretched his wings out wide, feeling the warm air rising underneath him, pushing him gently upwards and he angled his tail feathers and body to spin lazily in ever widening circles, high above the land, with nothing above him but the blue sky and the distant, burning sun.

This was what he was meant to be doing. This was what he was supposed to be. This.

Or so he thought

Being a vulture and flying was wonderful: It *was* peaceful, it *was* tranquil. The Onion Man loved circling high above the ground, rippling in a heat haze beneath him, silently spinning in wide circles on the rising thermal currents of air; weaving in and out between the other silently gliding vultures, simultaneously gave him a sense of camaraderie and freedom.

The problem was that when it came to food, he and the other vultures spent a lot of time with their heads and necks deep inside the bloated corpses of animals that had been dead too long in the hot Indian sun. The heat, the smell, the flies and the mess was more than he could bear.

No … this wouldn't do.

The freedom, the peace and the tranquility were increasingly marred by the knowledge that sooner or later he would be using his sharp beak to burrow deep into the flyblown innards of some unfortunate beast.

* * *

One evening, as twilight approached, instead of roosting on a sturdy branch somewhere, the Onion Man flew back to the city.

As the setting sun turned the sandstone walls from a light ochre to a blushing russet and the air began to cool, and the city lulled as its workers returned home to rest or prepare for the evening, the Onion Man heard strains of music and singing, coming from the direction of the palace.

He hopped off the wall and beat his big wings strenuously against the air, propelling him up, towards the place where the music was emanating. Settling on the stone railing of a balcony, his keen vulture eyes peered through the holes in the pierced screens that covered the windows.

The room beyond was already lit with lamps; sumptuous furniture and drapes decorated the room and waves of incense wafted out. Around the edges of the room a number of richly dressed men were reclining on couches and cushions, while a flute and sitar player accompanied the singing and dancing of the most beautiful woman he'd ever seen: Her eyes flashed; bells tinkled on her ankles as she stepped and stamped; delicate gold jewelry adorned her hands, fingers, tow, throat, forehead and a chain as fine as a strand of silk ran from a piercing in her nose to her ear; her graceful fingers curled backwards and then snapped together, ringing the little cymbals tied to them, and she sang with a voice like a morning bird.

Oh, how he wished he could be one of those men, luxuriating and watching the captivating performer.

He watched for an hour or more until the woman and her musicians finally finished, to scattered applause from the opulent audience. As night fell and the stars began to come out, like the diamonds the rich men wore on rings or studded their turbans, the Onion Man spread his wings and, for the last time, drifted to the tree where he and the other vultures roosted, and slept until morning woke him.

'* * *

As soon as the sun had peeped above the horizon he hopped onto the ground and, with his curved, sickle-beak he grasped his breast and pulled. And as he pulled, his feathered skin came away and floated off, turning to dust on the wind.

He straightened up, now a man once more, but dressed in finery – in silks and brocades, his brightly coloured turban pinned at the front with a grass-green jewel and a tall feather.

How grand he looked as he swaggered in through the city gate, the guards bowing to him in reverence, his left arm swinging by his side, his right hand resting on the handle of a jewel-pommelled sword.

He felt very comfortable in his new skin – women wrapped veils over their faces and peeped coyly at him and men stared admiringly as he strode through the city, noting the old place where he used to play his tablas. Innkeepers invited him to take refreshing drinks under cooling canopies, for free, so that other well-to-do customers would see him patronising their establishments and come to purchase their own drinks and refreshments.

What he didn't notice was the jealous men and women who peered at him through squinted eyes, or curled their lips in scorn, or cursed him for his good fortune.

And it was a group of these men who followed him down the street, at a distance, until he turned into a quieter alley and rushed up and surrounded him. They told him to hand over his money and, when he said he had none – for this was true – they became ugly and pointed their weapons at him. He drew his sword, but they laughed at its delicate construction and how he held it, showing he was clearly not used to using it, and demanded he take off his rich clothes as they would now take everything from him.

But this ... he gladly agreed to.

He unbuttoned his silken jacket, took hold of one side and pulled, throwing the garment away and letting it to turn to dust in the air.

And now the gang of thieves balked and quailed as, where the defenceless rich man had stood, there now towered a mighty bear!

While they stood frozen, their jaws gone slack and their eyes popping, the Onion Man roared the great bellowing roar of a bear and swiped at the gang, knocking three of the men flying.

Recovering themselves, the battered thieves and their comrades fled in all directions, crying out for help and shouting for the city guard.

The Onion Man, feeling very satisfied with himself, dropped to all fours and wondered what he would do next, only to find that within moments the city guard did arrive! Clustered together and holding their long spears in front of them they cautiously advanced on the Onion Man.

He tried to explain that no one was in any danger and, in fact, he had just defended himself from a gang of cutthroats who'd tried to rob him of everything he owned, but it came out as a rolling, bestial garbled burbling noise that only served to alarm the guards even more.

Desperate to save himself but not hurt any of the men who were, after all, doing their duty and protecting the people of the city, he rose onto his hind legs once more and roared a mighty roar that shook the walls of the buildings around him, bringing stones and dust raining down.

The guards backed up and clustered together even more, out of fear, but before they had a chance to rally themselves and present a phalanx of lethal spearheads, the Onion Man, on all fours again, galloped, in that loping way bears have, away from the guards and towards the city gates, roaring as he went, so that the streets cleared in front of him, with people ducking into doorways or climbing polls to escape the seemingly enraged animal. Meeting no resistance at the gates, the Onion Man ran straight out of the city.

Stopping to catch his breath, the Onion Man wiped tears from his furry cheeks and sat on the floor in the shade of a tower on the city walls, feeling very sorry for himself.

He had been driven from his home to live on the streets of the city, been chased away by monkeys, scavenged rotting meat as a vulture, been robbed by brigands and now chased by soldiers. He *was* in sorry state and sobbed into his big bear paws.

* * *

As the morning sun climbed to midday and the shadow he was resting in shrank to a knife-edge, the Onion Man decided to move off.

Slowly and sadly, with no direction in mind he got to his four feet and started walking, but almost instantly bumped into something on the floor that made a loud, metallic clanking noise.

Looking down he saw his old tablas that he'd abandoned here, when he'd first decided to stop being a musician and instead become a monkey. The bodies of the instruments were still very serviceable, but the drum skins on both had been punctured and torn.

He looked at the sad little drums and missed them. He missed his old life as a tabla player and came to a decision: His constant search for a life that was bigger, better, that had more of this or more of that, and changing his skin was over. He decided to be the man he had been born to be and be the best of that man that he could be.

So, for one last time, and with his great curved claws in his bear paw, he caught hold of the skin on his chest and pulled.

The bear's skin came away like a silk scarf from a woman's cheek, but this time, instead of throwing it to the wind to become dust, he held onto it.

He was now a man once more – and the man he'd been born to be, dressed in modest but well cut clothes, suitable for a successful musician, his aspect handsome, but not proud.

He took the bearskin and, with the aid of a small knife scraped the fur off, cut it to size and stretched it tight over the tablas.

He was a good tabla player and, remembering the musicians and the singer from last night, he straightened his jacket and walked on up to the Maharaja's palace, where he knocked at one of the servants' entrances and enquired after the performers.

After a brief conversation and a short audition, in the evening of the very same day he found himself drumming, alongside the flute and sitar players, as the woman sang and danced, much to the pleasure of their affluent audience, who rewarded them all handsomely.

From that day on, the Onion Man never changed his skin again. He was also never again known as the Onion Man, but people called him by his birth name. As time passed, he honed his skill as a tabla player ever further, until people came to seek him out and learn from him, and he lived a fulfilling and prosperous life … just as himself.

#0143 - 221018 - C0 - 210/148/5 - PB - DID2335915